Dug Up

Erica Hart

ISBN:9798325361098

DEDICATION

I'd like to thank Grim Poppy Designs for my fantastic cover art and also David Smith and Carl Hancock for helping with my research for this novella.

CONTENTS

TRIGGER WARNINGS!!

This book is very dark and deals with extremely sensitive subject matter.
If you are easily offended, please do not read this book!!

1 THE COLDNESS OF THE FLESH

My childhood was a lot different to the majority of people. I grew up surrounded by the dead. My father was a mortician in a little North American town called Bridgeworth. It was a quaint, sleepy place near the sea, and we lived in a big house attached to the funeral home next to Willow Park Cemetery. He was one in a long line of morticians, with the business being passed from father to son for generations.

Graveyards are amazing places to play hide and seek in, and Willow Park was ginormous dotted with yew and oak trees, some hundreds of years old. I was always told not to play near the very old graves because the ground there was unstable, and Father Gregory had even fenced off part of the cemetery for being too precarious.

The church stood overlooking the cliff. It was an

impressive gothic structure with stained glass windows that shone intricate coloured patterns on the ground when the sunlight hit them.

Father Gregory was a dirty old man. He made me feel uncomfortable. He was unfortunate looking with frizzy grey hair, mottled skin, a paunch and floppy jowls that made him talk with a lisp. He often smelt of the server wine. He would hold my hand a little too long when he was saying “Peace be with you” or brush past my rear inappropriately.

Mother had a good rapport with him though when organising the funeral services, flower arrangements and such.

I was always an introverted child and that hadn’t altered as I reached my teens. I never felt like I fitted in with any of the cliques at school and was a loner. I never thought I was a good-looking boy even though I was built quite well, but facially I was non-descript with my dark hair and brown eyes. I was dull I suppose. I did however have one talent; I could talk to the dead.

It was during my thirteenth year that the dead spoke to me for the first time.

My father often had me helping him, believing that my schooling was just a formality and didn’t mean anything since my calling was to take over the business when he was no longer able. He showed me everything he knew, becoming my teacher. I

learnt about embalming and preparing the bodies to be viewed by the family, applying make- up so that they were presentable and looked alive so as not to upset their loved ones. In all honesty I preferred the company of the dead. They didn't complain or make me feel awkward for not being popular enough.

One balmy evening in July, we'd had a particularly trying day with a lot of bodies coming in. Just past 7pm, a young girl was dropped off. We took her out of the body bag and laid her out on the metal table.

"Bryce just cover her over will you and we will deal with her tomorrow," said my father as he rubbed his eyes.

"I will after I finish mopping," I said, feeling tired and looking forward to mother's meat loaf.

"Good boy. Don't be too long. You know your mother doesn't like to be kept waiting to dish up dinner." He left me to finish up. I loved being here on my own. It was so quiet, so peaceful.

I fetched a clean sheet from the laundry basket to cover up the naked girl. She was only about sixteen, with long wavy auburn hair. She was beautiful and her pendulous breasts betrayed her young years. There were cuts running up her arms from her wrists. That must be how she lost her life.

I felt something happen in my boxers; my dick was throbbing. That was when I heard it.

“Do you like my body Bryce?” I froze and dropped the sheet, looking around the room to see where the voice was coming from. When I turned back the girl was sat up and her eyes were open. They were a vivid green.

“Are you still alive?” I breathed, terrified.

“I am to you because you’re special and you can hear me,” she said, her voice sweet and lilting. I poked my head out of the room looking up the dimly lit hall, straining my ears to make sure that my father had definitely left.

“You like my big tits don’t you?” she said suggestively. My mouth was dry, and I could feel the perspiration running down my neck.

“They’re amazing. Can I touch them?” I said, my hand outstretched.

“MMM yes baby, touch them and let me see that little cock get rock solid.” She lay back down and smiled. I trembled as I touched her tit. The skin was cold and the nipples stiff. I felt my cock leap to attention.

“Kiss me. Oh, baby you’re making my cunt wet,” she moaned, and I bent over the table and kissed her entangling my tongue with her limp one and tasting a hint of blood which excited me even more. My dick was straining against my underwear, and I rubbed it as I French kissed her, groping her fantastic tits with my other hand. My hand began to

wander down her body until it met her fuzzy muff. The copper pubic hair was nearly trimmed into a perfect little triangle. I stroked her clit, a little unsure as this was my first time touching a girl. The little knub felt like a frozen pea. I spread her delicious folds and gazed in wonder at her pink vaginal cavity. Clear liquid was drizzling out of her, and I felt the intense hunger to put my erect dick deep inside.

"You want to fuck me like you've seen father do to mother don't you?" she said her body pleading for pleasure. I had often spied on my parents when they were having sex. My mother was a bit of a screamer, and her moaning would wake me up. I would slowly open the door a little to see my dad ramming his fat todger into mum's gaping cunt. I had my first wank session watching them when I was about nine. A few drops of milky white cum ebbed out as I saw my father pull out of mum, leaving her cunt lips hanging open and his seed spilling out.

I never thought I'd be able to find a willing pussy at my age who was hungry for my virgin dick. I pulled down my pants and clambered on top of the girl and slid my hot manhood inside her cold clam. She began to whisper in ecstasy.

"Oh yes that's it! Fuck me! Deeper!"

I rammed my rampant cock deep inside her womb and felt the cold grip of her vaginal walls squeezing

me like a vice. After a couple of pumps, I felt my dick erupt and my face flush, a lightheaded feeling overtaking me. I'd lost my virginity to this undead goddess. I pulled out of her, and my semen and her blood leaked out all over the table. Panicked, I cleaned her up and wiped my sticky cock, flinging the sheet over her as she smiled and giggled at me. I quickly dressed and switched the lights off.

That night as I lay in bed in the depths of darkness, I could hear her calling my name. My dick waggled with want.

2 ADDICTED TO DEAD BODIES

The ferocity at which my obsession with fucking the dead grew knew no bounds. I thirsted for the pallor of dead skin and the slight whiff of rot.

Dead men never spoke to me, and I assumed it was because the women wanted my company and the feel of my hot teen dick in their slits. They all begged to be fucked; a last earthly pleasure before being buried or burnt. Father was especially pleased that I stayed late a lot of the time since he thought I was brushing up on his teachings and familiarising myself with the business. But of course, it was dead matter that fuelled my after-work activities and I became particularly cranky if we didn't have any women brought in for a few days and my balls hung low, heavy and in need of release. It didn't matter to me the condition of the body or the age. A cunt was a cunt regardless. Just a receptacle for my muck.

One particular afternoon, an elderly woman was brought in. She had died two weeks previously and the body had been left to decompose in her flat. The pathologist said she died of natural causes. She smelt pretty fucking awful, but my need to ejaculate overcame my scent glands. Whilst father was embalming her, she turned her head sharply towards me giving me a toothless grin. Her skin was a green and yellow hue.

“Wait for daddy to go, then we can play!!” she cackled. I had quickly realised that my father couldn’t see or hear the corpses moving and talking, though the first time it happened in front of him I shit myself. At last father left for the night and I could feel myself salivating and the pre cum oozing from my cock. I removed the padding from her genitalia and went down on her putrid cunt.

“Oh yes you young pup,” she rasped, “get your tongue right in there!” The taste of disintegrated innards and piss filled my mouth, and I began to wretch.

“Swallow it! Swallow me! Taste my insides!” yelled the woman, riding the wave of pleasure. I pinched my nose and swallowed. I belched and a taste of rotten fish and spoiled meat filled my mouth. In spite of that, my dick was ready for action. The woman opened her scrawny legs and parted her grey pube covered labia. I inserted my pulsating dick in and groaned, the feeling of dead flesh wrapped around my cock was addictive. The cold

hole filled with decaying bodily fluids welcomed my blood engorged appendage like a hungry mouth. I could hear the woman murmuring dirty talk as I fucked her deeply and emptied into her. When I pulled out, my cock was dripping with semen and black goo.

"Put that cum soaked cock in my mouth," the old crone said, breathlessly. "I bet you've never been given head by someone with no teeth. Nothing sharp to hurt your cock, just gums and spit!" I shoved my damp, limp dick into her drooping mouth and rode her face slowly. My cock began to stiffen when I saw her crinkled, age spotted jowls slap around my shaft. The woman's eyes flew open and fluttered as I gave her throat a thick, creamy load.

As I had done so many other times before, I cleaned her up and went home. The bodies were always silent for a while after I'd given them my seed. But later on, the voices would always haunt my dreams.

My hunger for the embrace of the dead took over my life. My mother said as much one evening whilst we were having dinner. She said that Summer was nearly over, and I should be out with my friends instead of being cooped up sorting out dead bodies.

I shrugged it off saying I was happy doing my work, which made my father beam with pride. I also didn't have the heart to tell my mother that I had no

friends and was a social outcast.

“He’s a natural Valerie. He’s coming on in leaps and bounds. Pretty soon he will be able to embalm a body all by himself,” said my father grinning. I felt a warm rush of happiness. It felt good to be praised. If only he knew what I really did. I felt my happiness turn to shame and I looked down at my half-eaten plate of macaroni cheese.

There was a lull at the funeral parlour for a couple of weeks and dad said it was because in Summer lots of people were away on holiday. We had a heatwave as well and it was sweltering beyond belief. We put oscillating fans in the funeral home in the chapel of rest, and it was lucky that father had installed air conditioning where the bodies were kept, else the smell would have been something fierce. The heat didn’t help my libido; it increased it tenfold. My nerve endings twitched for the feel of frigid skin and the smell of a freshly expired body beneath my trembling lips and fingers.

Presently, there was a young woman brought in who had been in a house fire. There was a leaky gas pipe and when she switched on the light, the house was engulfed. She looked like she had been skinned. Her flesh was sticky and wet and charred to black in places. She had no eyes, ears or lips and gave off an aroma of bacon sandwiches.

“Oh, Bryce I can’t wait to feel your hands all over my burnt body!!” crowed the corpse. I laughed

inanely.

“This is no laughing matter Bryce. This body is obviously not having a viewing. They want a quick funeral. She is to be buried next door in the cemetery. The family felt that cremating her would have been in bad taste,” said my father, gravely. The cadaver howled with mirth, bile and blood dribbling from the blackened hole that was once a mouth. I held in a laugh, not really knowing why it was funny.

“My cunt is cooked to perfection; hot and juicy ready for you baby,” said the woman, masturbating her clit with crispy fingers. I half listened to my father as my penis whirled around in my pants like a windmill. This girl was my test. Father said that sometimes you had to embalm bodies that were badly damaged. I asked why since no one was even going to see it only us and he said that was just the way of things. I felt a little nervous especially since she was begging me over and over to impale her with my cock. I gently washed the blistered body and delicately performed the embalming process, even though there was precious little left of her organs.

“Well done my boy,” father said, clasping my shoulder. I covered her over.

“Don’t be long Brycey baby. My gash is seeping juice and needs to feel you in it,” said the girl, her voice muffled under the sheet.

Father and I then wheeled Mr. Phelps to the chapel of rest and laid him out in his coffin. He looked dapper in a light blue suit.

The dead looked serene and at peace when ensconced in their coffins. A far cry from how I felt as of late with the women speaking to me constantly. I swore if I listened very closely, I could hear a faint voice beckoning me from the churchyard. I couldn't understand how that could be. They were buried now and should be on the next part of their journey to oblivion. I couldn't sleep because of the constant buzzing in my head, so I tried stuffing my ears with cotton wool, but the voices just got louder, so now my go to method for getting some shut eye was to have a snifter of father's Jim Bean laced with sleeping pills. It gave me a quiet night of dreamless sleep. I always awoke starving and was glad of mom's scrumptious breakfasts. Sometimes pancakes and other times waffles with bacon and there was always freshly squeezed juice. Mom loved that I had such a hearty appetite and I kept lean from riding my bike or walking down the stone steps to the beach. I loved breathing in the salty air and watching the waves crash on the jagged dark grey rocks. Even that far away from the funeral parlour I could still hear them. My constant hard dick was making me weary.

I pulled myself out of my thoughts as I vacuumed the cherry red carpet and dead headed the flowers

from the displays next to Mr. Phelps' coffin. Dad came in as I was putting the vacuum in the closet.

"I have to pop into town. When you've finished, give your mom a hand with dinner," he said, waving as he left.

As soon as he was gone, I went back to the burnt girl. I lifted the sheet, and she gave me a gooey, lipless smile.

"I love that you will be fucking me in front of all of the other men," she said, running her crispy hands across her blistered tits. I glanced over at the three sheeted bodies; a cancer victim, man who'd died of a heart attack and someone who had been fatally stabbed by a jealous lover.

"You like to be watched then?" I said, bemused.

"Oh, yes! I love seeing men get turned on by seeing me being fucked. I'm a dirty little slut on the sly!" I belly laughed and touched her cheek. She felt moist. I rubbed my fingers together and licked them. It tasted salty and bitter. I pulled down my trousers and my restrained dick flopped out. When I removed the wadding, it was heavy with burnt blood and serum from the burst blisters inside her vaginal canal. I suddenly felt primal and frenzied and threw my erection into her. The labia began to disintegrate as I pummelled her hole, but this only made me go deeper. The sight of gore and the grotesqueness of it all had a profound effect on me

and made me harder still. The young woman screamed my name as I climaxed, and I shit myself when I pulled out of her bringing half her intestines with me. Her pelvic area had been reduced to lumpy meat.

“Fuck!” I said, not knowing how I was going to fix this mess. The girl began to laugh, jeering at me. I backhanded her sharply.

“What are you going to tell your daddy now?” she teased.

“Shut up!!! Just shut up!!” I screamed, banging my knuckles on the side of my head.

I hastily shoved everything back inside and bunged her up with some fresh wadding. Then I cleaned her and myself up, realising I had knocked a chunk out of her cheek when I slapped her. I found it under the table so dried it off and stuck it back to her face with some superglue out of the desk drawer.

She kept laughing and I could hear it even when I got home. I asked to be excused from dinner. I had lost my appetite.

“Are you ill Bryce?” said my mother concerned.

“No mom. I’m just tired. I have been working late quite a bit. I just need to sleep,” I said, just wanting to get to the safety of my room.

“Now Bryce, your mother has worked hard preparing this meal. It’s disrespectful to leave your food,” said father, his voice stern.

“It’s OK Edward. I will make him up a plate. He can have it later.” Mom smiled sympathetically at me as I made a sharp exit before father could scold me some more.

I got in the shower and washed myself angrily. That bitch laughed at me and all of a sudden I could hear her as well as all of the other kids who picked on me at school all laughing, all at once.

“You are a weirdo living in that creepy house…Your dad is Dr Death!” they would say. The jibes were tough, and I hated people making me into the butt of their jokes. I had fucked a lot of corpses in the last two years, but none had disrespected me like that cooked slut had. They need my jism to put life into their dead husks and who would they talk to if I wasn’t there? Who would fuck them and listen to them moan as their rotten insides absorbed my milk?

That night there were too many voices; it reached fever pitch and even my “lights out” cocktail didn’t work, so I ran into the wall and smashed my head into it to knock myself out.

3 NEW LIFE

Mother was worried when she found me concussed on the bedroom floor. I said I had tripped and hit my head, a lie which she readily believed. My smashed head made me have dizzy spells and bouts of nausea, so mother made me stay home for a few days. The chattering stopped and it felt strange to hear no noise only silence.

By mid-September I had returned to school. The women it seems, were ignoring me. Maybe they just had nothing to say. I didn't even feel like fucking. It was like that bump on my head had reset my libido to zero.

One Thursday evening, we sat down to dinner and mother excitedly announced her pregnancy. The preparations for the birth became the focus of my life. I helped paint the nursery; mom was having a girl, so we put all twinkly pink and white lights

across the ceiling and I helped father assemble the wooden crib. My perverse antics seemed a forgotten memory and that sentiment increased even more after Amelia was born. She was the light of my life. I realised that my purpose was to look after her and be a good example. I found myself spending minimal time in the funeral parlour and more time with Amelia, and even on the days I went to work, especially after mother had finished her maternity leave, I took Amelia with me. We set up a play pen in the chapel of rest where we could keep our eye on her. Even father loved his daughter being around. I got on with my work efficiently and diligently so I could get done and go and take Amelia for a walk or read her stories. There was still no chit chat. I thought my curse had been broken and now I could be normal and happy.

Mom said that I'd make a great father one day and my dad agreed. He said it was good to see me smile and enjoy my life. Due to my new unfettered mind, I graduated with decent grades. Then it was time to join father in running the business. I worked hard and enjoyed my work, especially liaising with clients to find a particular piece of music they wanted to make the goodbyes easier.

Amelia was growing into a very bright girl. She started school and loved being the centre of attention. She was a chatty, cheeky little madam with a smattering of freckles across her nose, glossy brown curls and violet eyes. Unusual and

ethereal looking. I always said that she was an angel sent to cure me. She loved walking around the graveyard and her favourite place was near the angel headstones that overlooked the cliff. We would set up a picnic blanket there on the grass and Amelia would draw with her box of coloured crayons whilst I played my harmonica.

Father Greogory was always surveying Amelia with beady little black eyes like he was appraising a calf to see if it was fit for market. I never left him alone with her. I knew he was evil, a follower of the devil in priest's vestments.

"I don't like him," said Amelia, as she finished one of her drawings. It was Father Gregory in the form of a pig. I chuckled. "He smells funny, and he has bad breath."

"Don't worry I won't let Father Piggery hurt you," I said, ruffling her curls. She giggled, taking a bite of one of the apples we had picked from the tree in the back garden. The juice ran down her chin and she wiped it with the back of her hand. She jumped up then, wanting to play hide and seek behind the big crypts, another favourite game. Then like most days, we would make our way down the seventy stone steps to the beach, where Amelia would run along the shoreline, squealing because the water was so cold.

"When you're a bit bigger we will get you armbands and we can go in the water and I'll teach you to

swim," I said, as we sat on the warm sand watching the sky turn pink.

"OOOOHH Pretty.." Amelia said, yawning.

"Come on, get on my back. Mother will be expecting us for dinner." I carried her back up the steps, feeling her little arms holding onto me. I felt proud and honoured to care for this child's life.

On Amelia's sixth birthday that June, we had a barbecue. Mom and I decorated the yard with fairy lights and bunting. Twenty children arrived dressed in their best party outfits. The girls in satin and frills and the boys in braces and smart trousers. We had a girl doing face painting and Amelia had a pink butterfly painted on her cheek in glitter. I, of course was in charge of the party games, so we did pass the parcel and musical statues and father manned the barbecue serving delicious sausages and burgers whilst mother kept the parents entertained and made gin cobblers and Pimm's. Father Gregory turned up with a present for Amelia, a pink, leather-bound bible. I scowled at him then turned my attention back to the kids hitting the piñata.

A little later on, Bradley, one of the boys came out of the house crying, followed closely by Father Gregory who was red faced and dishevelled. He ran to his mom, a plump woman who was enjoying an onion laden hotdog.

"Mommy I want to go home," he snivelled, tears

running down his face.

"Can I finish this, then we will go," she said, disappointed.

"Hey Bradley," I said, "do you want to get your face painted?" The boy rushed towards me and grabbed my hand. "Why are you so upset?" I said as we walked away.

"Father Gregory frightened me," Bradley said, but wouldn't elaborate on how.

I made up my mind then and there to expose Father Gregory for the despicable fool he was. Scaring kids and being creepy definitely wasn't godly.

We began to spend more time together as a family. Even father wasn't cooped up with the dead like he used to be. We went away camping for the weekend and Amelia loved toasting marshmallows on the open fire whilst father strummed his guitar. Mother taught her how to press flowers in a book and we took some walking trails that led high up into the mountains where the view was breathtaking and the air clean and crisp.

My parents looked healthy and content; mom had rosy cheeks, her brown hair glistened, and her grey eyes sparkled. And father, who always looked so stern and sinister, was now smiling and his greying hair was cut in a new trendy style. Amelia had saved us all.

One late August afternoon, Amelia and I were in our usual spot having a picnic on a patchwork blanket. We had just finished eating some tasty cheese salad sandwiches on homemade bread. The sun was warm, but not stifling, and I told Amelia not to wander as I closed my eyes for a moment, leaving her to press some wildflowers in the new flower press that dad had bought her.

"Bryce look! It's a butterfly!" Amelia giggled, happily. She jumped up and ran after it.

"Amelia, wait up," I said as I rubbed my eyes groggily. The little girl skipped along right towards the fenced off area of the churchyard. The butterfly with it's beautiful red and yellow wings landed atop of one of the crumbling tombstones. Amelia, not concerned with danger, ducked under the fence, raising her tiny hand towards the beautiful creature.

That's when the ground gave way and she screamed.

"Amelia! Amelia! You know you're not meant to go in there!" I scolded hurtling over the fence. The colour drained from my face as I looked into the 6-foot-deep hole. Amelia's body had landed at an uncomfortable angle. She had fell through the rotted coffin and the rib bones of the occupant had pierced her little body. Blood oozed from her mouth and her eyes were open staring at me in terror. I howled in anguish.

The butterfly flew away.

4 DOWNWARD SPIRAL

I stood numbly, watching as Amelia's coffin was lowered into the ground. Father Gregory droned on about the importance of taking each day as it comes and how life can be snuffed out in the blink of an eye. But the loss of a child although tragic, was all part of God's plan.

Really.

Letting children die needlessly while dirty old priests prey on the innocent. I steadily lost my faith, not that I really had any to begin with anyways. I thought it was all a croc of shit.

The attendees shuffled away; their heads bowed. Like you even gave a fuck about my sister. You didn't spend time braiding her hair or stroking her back to sleep when she had a nightmare. Funerals to me were so fucking hypocritical. It never struck me how much until I was here watching my kid sister be buried. People turned up to pay their respects even though they didn't give a fuck about you when you were alive, so they can feel like the good Samaritan. Well, fuck off I don't need your fucking sympathy. Your pity won't bring her back. I therefore decided to stay with Amelia even though mom had put a spread on back at the house. I watched as the excavator filled in the hole, my heart breaking with each shovelful of earth. Never

again would I hear her sing or giggle. Never again would I see her smile that lifted you even when you felt like shit.

Once the excavator had left, I lay on the soil and listened to see if I could hear her. Nothing, only painful silence. I felt myself drift away into a kind of half sleep, finding comfort in being near her. When I came fully around, it was dark. My parents hadn't come looking for me. They left me to deal with the grief in my own way, too preoccupied with their own feelings. That was when I heard it. The distinct call of my name. I cocked my head to the side, trying to ascertain where the sound was coming from. Sadly it wasn't Amelia, but it was coming from the dilapidated part of the cemetery. I had no inkling to revisit the scene of my sister's death, but the sudden desire between my legs overtook me. My jaw tightened as I climbed over the fence. I peered into the hole and the skeleton was laughing, its bony legs akimbo, touching where its tits should have been. I descended into the hole, its voice becoming a crescendo of pleading to be used. The smears of Amelia's blood were still visible on its broken ribs.

"Innocent blood that woke me after all these years. I can smell your seed young man. Come, give me that sweet milk that I've been craving!" cackled the skeleton, its bones cracking as it turned its head to look at me with eyeless sockets. I glanced up at the head stone, squinting to see the inscription in the

moonlight. Her name was Augustine Mellor and she had died in 1849.

Suddenly, as if my curse had been cast tenfold, I feverishly began to pull my pants down to free my girthy member. The skeleton opened its mouth as I rammed my dick in, the teeth cutting my shaft, making it bleed. My brow was perspiring as I thrust my manhood into the skeletal mouth, and I felt worms dropping on me from where they had disturbed the earth either side of the hole to remove Amelia's body. Bugs crawled all over my nether regions, but I was lost in the moment. The embrace of the dead enveloping me once more. The skull began to split, and I felt my cock butt against the rotted base of the coffin. Splinters jabbed into my helmet, but I kept on, desperate to feel the wave of my impending orgasm. It erupted, filling the remains of the skull with a thick bloody goop. The bugs were swimming in it, and I laughed dirtily to myself. The skeleton had stopped speaking now since there wasn't much left of it. I stood up and angrily jumped on the ribs that had killed my sister. Then I hoisted myself out. My cock, although bleeding and wounded, still wasn't satiated. Fuck drunk, I staggered as I pulled up my pants. I could hear a thousand women's voices calling to me. I covered my ears, the noise giving me a headache and that familiar ringing in my ear canal.

"Shut up! I am one man. Please stop calling all at once!!" I felt like I had been struck by lightning and

wandered in a daze of torment and arousal to the shed behind the church. It was annoyingly locked. After checking in the nearby parked excavator, I didn't find any keys, so I picked up a rock and smashed the padlock. Inside was a vast array of tools that Max the groundskeeper and gravedigger used. I picked up a sharp shovel and went back into the graveyard. I tried to pick out a distinct tone from all of the noise, then I found one.

"Bryce! Over here! Dig me up!" she said in a soft, sensual whisper that made my dick stand up, blood pumped. The earth was still quite soft so she must have only been here a few months. I began to dig with purpose, the mounds of earth piling up on either side of the growing hole. Eventually, once I was weary and dripping with sweat, I hit the top of the coffin. I brushed the last few bits of soil away and tried to open it. It wouldn't budge. I used the sharp end of the shovel, thankful for the full moon that bathed me in an eerie glow and enabled me to see what I was doing. The coffin lid popped open, nearly knocking me out.

The girl was heavily decomposed, laying surrounded by stained pink satin. The coffin flies buzzed around the decomposed flesh, feeding off her rotten remains. She smiled at me, the black rotted blood oozing from her mouth. The side of her face had wasted away and the white communion style dress she was wearing was torn and covered with her expunged bodily fluids.

With trembling hands, I lifted her dress and straddled her, not even grimacing at the smell of dead meat. Her thighs were covered in a waxy like substance and I removed the heavy, stained wadding and rammed my cock into her cunt. It squelched as puss and festered matter leaked all over my dick and balls. My sense of smell betrayed me, and I threw up all over her, giggling like a kid and rubbing the lumpy, brown vomit into her tits. I emptied my protein into her and kissed her ruined mouth, hearing her sigh contentedly, the taste of rot and decay made me vomit again all over her face. I laughed wildly as I climbed out of the hole, picking some grubs out of my teeth. I was glad I was just over six foot tall, else I would have struggled getting out without a ladder.

Exhausted and covered in mud and other unknown substances, I wandered home, the humming of the voices becoming almost soothing. I flung open the kitchen door, realising that my parents were in bed. It must've been the middle of the night by now. I trudged muddy footprints all over the grey tiled floor, but I didn't give a fuck. I pulled open the cutlery drawer and took out a steak knife. I went upstairs to the bathroom and ran a hot bath putting plenty of bubbles in. Amelia loved bubble baths. We would always play bubble dress princesses and I would place handfuls of the bubbles onto her skin, making them into a gown fit for a princess much to her amazement. I punched the side of the bath angrily. I stripped and sunk into the steaming water

letting it cleanse and soothe my aching body.

I could still hear them all. Begging, pleading, demanding, then getting angry because I was ignoring them. I picked up the knife and slid the blade vertically down my wrist, the blood dribbling slowly, then speeding up. The muttering got louder. I could swear they were in the room with me. Then I heard my mother's voice. It seemed further away. I felt like I was wrapped in cotton wadding.

"Bryce, who are you talking to in there? Open the door! Why have you trodden mud all through the house?!"

I tried to answer but I felt like I was floating. Then everything went black.

5 MY DIRTY LITTLE SECRET

My double life started when Amelia was around two years old. I would go on my jaunts to town to run errands or buy things for dinner. I was a pretty respected guy in our neighbourhood, being that I dealt with everyone's loved ones and gave them a good send off, so no one would ever have known what I was really doing when I was let loose in the concrete jungle.

Hidden sites on the internet gave me the information and paraphernalia I needed to indulge in my fantasies. It just took a while before I was finally given an address to act on them for real.

The location was unassuming and discreet down a non-descript street off the main drag. That's where Mason had his bordello. Only his was slightly different than others because the oldest hooker was thirteen.

I'd known Mason ever since he sang in the church choir, in fact his parents still attended Father Gregory's services. Mason was a ginger haired, strapping lad who started up this joint just after he turned nineteen and got his inheritance from his grandma. He too liked young flesh and was very good at getting them to do the job willingly. They all related to him because he was pretty cool; he rode a Harley. He let them smoke weed and drink bourbon. A lot of the kids were runaways, but some of them had been kidnapped and "broken" before they were handed to Mason.

Of course, Mason's parents had no clue what he was doing. He said he was running a hospice for wayward kids, a laughable lie. He was also pushing high grade weed. I swear this lad could charm the pants off anyone who crossed his path.

The first time I went there I nervously knocked three times as I was told to, and Mason let me in. He led me through the dimly lit burgundy hallway, with its gold leaf wallpaper to his office. Then he sparked up a joint and poured me a bourbon on the rocks.

"So, what are you looking for?" he said, blowing a smoke ring.

"I have a horrible secret," I said, relief washing over me at finally being able to offload to somebody, "I'm sexually attracted to my daughter. I know I'm going to hell, but I need some form of release. I don't

Mason became a friend and confidante and one day he told me about the other partner in his business- Father Gregory.

Mason had been molested by him from an early age. Father Gregory had a “breaking room,” a torture chamber in the catacombs of the church. He would take children there and abuse them. Mason however didn’t break. The torture made him stronger. In fact he thrived on it and as he grew up realised that he liked the deviant lifestyle and could make some serious bucks out of it, so him and Father Gregory had this trafficking situation going on. Some of the kids had families who were patrons of the church, so they were harder to kidnap and there were only so many runaway stories that they could fabricate. But Father Gregory still had his fun and tamed them, grooming them “For God,” hoping they would be mentally scarred and return to the hands of their abuser freely. Most did. Some ended up going mad. Father Gregory didn’t traumatise every kid that came into the church. He was selective and chose those that he thought would be attractive to clients and would make the most money.

I knew there was something up with that old bastard. Bryce had always told me about his inappropriate touching. I’m glad he never made moves on my boy, but then I suppose it was too close to home. You don’t shit on your own doorstep. The authorities never looked into it

"Told you he'd get used to it," Mason said, wanking himself off. My orgasm filled his guts to the brim, my spunk dribbling out looking pearlescent against his olive skin. I pulled out, my dick covered in clots and shit.

"My turn!" chirped Mason, ramming his big cock in. "Glad you warmed him up for me. Jesus he's still tight. He will make us a fortune." Mason fucked Javier hard, slapping his ass cowboy style, whilst I cleaned myself up and shakily lit a cigarette. Mason groaned as he ejaculated. However when he withdrew, he brought the boy's innards with him. We had ruptured his insides. Mason turned him over and saw the glassy eyed stare of death.

"Well Shit! At least we had a ride of him." Mason lamented.

"What are you going to do with him now?" I asked, zipping myself up.

"Ah! That brings us to the next part of our operation-body disposal." Mason wrapped Javier in the thick duvet and took us down to the basement. The cellar stunk like the funeral home did, of dead bodies. We walked along a stone corridor and at the end in front of some metal doors was a container of sorts with a lid. He opened it and I saw the partially decomposed face of the girl who I had seen the first time I came here. Mason threw Javier in.

"They usually come every week to take this, but it's not been emptied for two weeks because of the holidays. This is why it fucking stinks in here! Having men of influence who are clients means that someone comes to take the bodies to a landfill site, which is basically a mass grave, where they are then buried. No one will ever question it. They just do as they're told, they're well paid. All of their kid's college tuition is taken care of and they have a nice house and can keep their wives happy. The disposal of something that is already dead is a small price to pay for a life of luxury. Some of the kids don't last very long. The younger ones expire pretty quickly, but the older ones can last for a couple of years. I get rid of them when they're too loose from too much fucking- they're fucked fifteen times a day sometimes- and when their childlike innocence and tight openings have gone they have no use. If they don't die on the job, I poison their food. It's called streamlining the business. No money means their lives are over."

I really wish I'd never seen that to be honest, but I knew I had to continue my shady shenanigans. That was my price to pay for the perfect family- the perfect life.

6 BLESS ME FATHER FOR I HAVE SINNED

I haven't always been a man of the cloth; a devotee of the Lord. I was "normal" and dashingly good looking once. Happy even.

I had my first sexual encounter when I was eleven. It was with my stepbrother Mark who was twenty.

Whilst my mom and dad were out one evening and Mark was babysitting, he sneaked into my room when I was asleep and began groping my cock, whispering to me as I stirred not to tell our parents because I was special to him, and I made him hard. As he rubbed me, my little sausage got stiff. It excited me. I had always looked at boys and found them attractive, wondering why I didn't like girls. When the other boys brought in a Penthouse

I suppose Mark was my teacher in all things queer. He got some bootleg porn DVDS, and we would sit and watch them in his tiny flat near the beach and wank each other off which usually led to other things. He took my ass for the first time a couple of weeks later. He had a bottle of rush which he told me to sniff. I felt like my head was going to explode. Then he put thick lube on my hole and told me to relax, kissing me and mussing up my black hair. I bent over the bed, shivering as I thought it was going to hurt. He put the tip in at first to let my opening feel the girth of an adult penis. I groaned and pulled my ass cheeks open to let him enter. He slid slowly in, and I gasped with the pleasure and pain. It stung like fuck, but the feeling of having my anal cavity filled with a pulsating man's cock aroused me no end. I felt all grown up and in a different league to my classmates. He began to gently fuck my ass and I begged him to go faster, wanting to feel his jism filling me internally. When he came it felt wild and brazen. I was so embarrassed when he pulled out and his cock was covered in cum and shit.

"It's your first time. Next time I'll show you how to douche. Now I'll get you hard again and you do me. Let's see if you're top, bottom or versatile!" Mark laughed.

I was so knocked out I needed a break, so we did a couple of joints and listened to the new Bon Jovi LP. Mark took me into the bathroom, and we

liquor store trying to get some booze off any pervy old man that passed when Charlie saw me.

“What are you doing out here?” he asked, his smouldering good looks enchanting me.

“Trying to score some vodka,” I said, my cheeks flushing.

“I’ll get you some.” He winked and went into the store. Ten minutes later he returned with a bottle of vodka and a bottle of tequila. “Fancy some chasers?” he said, smiling warmly at me. In my fourteen and a half years I had never felt attraction or feelings like this before. I nodded and we went back to his place, a fancy town house near the cliffs. He had a balcony that overlooked the sea. The view was outstanding, and the sea air felt good in my lungs. I ended up blind drunk and of course we fucked many times that night. The next morning he asked if I had to go to school.

“I got expelled for smoking drugs behind the bleachers,” I laughed, “they caught me several times, but I didn’t give a fuck. Luckily they never found out that I sucked off the captain of the soccer team or my parents would’ve thrown me out.”

“Do you wanna make some serious money?” Charlie asked, propping himself up on his elbow.

“Sure. I’m broke. The job at the gas station washing cars pays fuck all,” I said, really wanting to fuck his ass again.

“I’m a pimp and I have a couple of boys who work for me, but none as hot as you. You can make a couple of hundred a day no problem.” I could feel his eyes on my crotch and felt my cock stiffen. I was a bit dubious but figured I’d give it a shot. Anything so I could spend more time with him. A couple of days later I started working for him. I took to it instantly. I loved sex and cock. I became Charlie’s top earner, and he would often invite me to his house, which he never did with the other boys. I tried cocaine with him for the first time just after my fifteenth birthday. My parents were happy that I had a job and could give them money to help with the bills. I told them I was a busboy down at the beach club. Glad of the extra income, they didn’t question me further.

Charlie told me he loved me one evening after I came back with a mega wad of cash and a sore ass. We plied our trade at carparks around town. Different ones every time so the police wouldn’t arrest us. Back at Charlie’s, he ran me a bath to let me soak my poor ass.

“I love you and I don’t want you to turn tricks anymore,” he said, lighting some candles next to the bath.

“What am I gonna do then?” I said, sinking into the steaming water gratefully.

“Help me recruit other boys and look after the ones we have and be my boyfriend. I don’t want anyone

else to touch you anymore. I want you to be mine and I yours." Charlie grinned, splashing me as I laughed.

This was the happiest point in my life. I moved in with Charlie and lived like a king, telling my parents that he was just my flat mate. They were bedazzled by him when he met them with his fancy clothes and suave persona.

The business was making us a lot of money and we were both developing quite the coke habit. High on hedonism, we were blind to the danger that lay ahead.

One balmy evening, we went out for a fish supper at a quaint little seafood restaurant near the bay. It was so romantic. We had a table on the terrace listening to the sound of the evening tide as the sun painted the sky in vibrant shades of pink and orange. We dined on lobster and crayfish and Charlie ordered some champagne. Afterwards we walked along the beach hand in hand, the stars beginning to sparkle in the sky. We made our way to the road to hail a cab and Charlie took me in his arms and kissed me.

"What an evening. You make me so happy you know. I think we should take a vacation soon. How about Hawaii or the Bahamas?" Heady will passion, I kissed him again, feeling like I was floating ten feet above the ground. That's when I felt something hard hit my head. Dazed, I turned and saw a group

of twenty-something lads shouting homophobic slurs at us. My head was bleeding profusely and Charlie, being the chivalrous fool he was, saw red. He spat at them and went to KO the culprit.

“Charlie leave it. Come on let’s go home,” I said, feeling woozy, but Charlie, fuelled with coke and champagne belligerently swung at one of the lads. Four on one, he had no chance. They leapt on him and began stamping on his head. I dashed into the fray, trying to pull them off him, but I too ended up getting a beating. Then I felt the blade in my side. I fell to the floor. Charlie wasn’t moving and his head was caved in. I could see his skull. The guys got spooked and I heard one of them say, “Fuck, I think he’s dead!” and I could feel my blood and Charlie’s pooling around me. I must’ve slipped into unconsciousness then because when I woke I was in a hospital bed with tubes coming out of me. My head and side hurt. I glanced to my left and saw my mother staring at me.

“Tell me it’s not true,” she said woefully, “that Charlie wasn’t a pimp. The policeman told us about him. They have had their eye on him for a while but have never had enough evidence to arrest him.”

“So, you’re not happy I’m still breathing after nearly getting killed? Where’s Charlie?” I said, trying to get out of bed but failing.

“Charlie’s dead,” said my mother in a monotone. I felt myself howl in pain, shocked that I could even

make such a pitiful sound.

“Charlie is the love of my life mom. Now you know. I’m gay,” I said, relieved at not having to lie anymore.

“Well there’s only one thing for it. You will need to spend time with God.” I tried to get out of bed again, but the nurse came rushing in.

“Tell me he’s not dead!” I wailed.

“I’m so sorry,” said the nurse gravely, “he was D.O.A and you’re lucky to be alive after being stabbed.” I went into shock screaming the place down. Then I felt myself slipping away as she gave me a sedative.

I spent two weeks in hospital, after which I was shipped off to a monastery up the coast where I was to learn the art of being a priest and offer my sorry homo life to God for cleansing and beg for forgiveness. I did try to escape a couple of times but was always brought back kicking and screaming and put in a locked room with nothing but a bible as company. In the end, I had to succumb and learn the ways of the church, or I’d never be allowed to leave. I began a dark journey into the depraved sins of the flesh and the devil, learning about God’s foe, feeling connected to him somehow. My mind began to split. All the good I had in me had left the day that Charlie died. There was nothing left but anger and the need to inflict

pain on the innocent, my jealousy for their uncomplicated, joy filled lives burning my soul. I wanted to destroy them all. Why should I have no happiness. Let them all die, never to feel bliss or gladness.

I left the monastery a well-respected priest, and my parents were proud as punch.

before it tore off limbs. Mason wouldn't be happy, but I'm sure we could find another little girl. I gathered the remains and put them in a wheelie bin which I then took to a pit down the way. The pit was my mass grave for the ones who didn't make it. I didn't use it often as we needed live kids to make money. I threw the girl into the pit and opened a nearby barrel, covering her in a few shovels of lye. The others down there had long ago decomposed and there were just a few bones scattered around. Finally they would all turn to dust and would never be found. I made my way back upstairs to organise getting some security cameras fitted in the churchyard since someone had been exhuming bodies and destroying the remains. I also had to work on my sermon for Sunday's service. Being a servant of God was a full-time job.

.

.

7 THE FRACTURED MIND

I woke up with a start. I was in hospital. Mom and dad were with me. Mom looked dog tired with dark circles under her eyes.

"Thank God you're awake," she said, tears streaming down her cheeks. Father stood silent near the doorway, the relief on his face palatable.

"Bryce my boy," he said in austere tone, "I know you miss Amelia, we all do, but your poor mother has been through enough. She doesn't need to lose a second child."

Somehow he made it all my fault. I knew my father loved me, but he was incapable of showing emotion and support when the going got tough.

"Baby, I wish you'd come home to be with us and grieve," my mom said, gently putting her head on my chest, trying to avoid the tubes that resembled

spaghetti junction.

I felt numb and drained. The mutterings were a mumbled indistinguishable whisper at present. I wish I'd succeeded. I couldn't take the noise anymore, nor the ceaseless arousal in my loins, needing to feel my cock in dead flesh. I knew I was fucked. My mind was lost to reason. But somewhere deep within, I questioned if it actually was real and they were speaking to me. What if I had been chosen by dark forces or some such to pleasure the dead and hear their last desires?

The nurse came in and checked my vitals.

"Why don't you two go home and get some rest? He is stable now. We will keep him comfortable, and I have a counsellor coming to see him tomorrow." My parents needed rest I suppose and I myself felt sleepy. I absentmindedly tugged at the bandages on my wrists and heard the faint sound of laughter.

The next day the counsellor came to speak to me but when she was talking her voice sounded all garbled so I couldn't understand what she was saying. It was like the voices didn't want me to hear her. They wanted me with them with no outside interference. I stared dead eyed straight ahead, feeling drool dribbling out of my mouth every so often. I wanted to wipe it, but my arms wouldn't move. The counsellor looked at me worriedly and wiped my mouth with a tissue. My mom was in the

hall, eagerly awaiting her diagnosis. Father was in work because he had a backlog, more so because of Amelia's funeral and I wasn't even there to help. I didn't really care about anything at this point. I just wanted to feel like I did when Amelia was alive- at peace.

I heard my mom in the hall sobbing.

"Your son has had a psychotic break," said the counsellor in a hushed voice, "I will give him some medication and recommend they keep him in here for monitoring for a couple of days. He needs complete rest and no stress. Take him out in nature to enrich him and help heal his mind and deal with his grief."

I closed my eyes, hearing a voice that had gotten louder amongst the low hum, calling me, enticing me. The repetitive whisper sent me to sleep.

In the middle of the night when I was sure I wasn't being watched, I slid out of bed, the floor freezing cold on my bare feet.

"Bryce, come downstairs. I'm waiting," said the women in a rasping whisper. The skeleton night staff didn't see me creep along the corridors. I got in the elevator and punched lower ground and it glided silently to its destination. The doors opened onto a dark corridor, dimly lit by flickering fluorescent lights. I padded down the hallway to the ominous double doors. The morgue. I cautiously

opened the door, checking for any signs of activity, but at 2am I doubted the coroner was going to be working. The coast was clear. It smelt like formaldehyde and my favourite aroma- decaying flesh. The voice was louder now. It was coming from one of the drawers. I flicked on the lights hearing them buzz and slid open the drawer. A curvy woman lay inside, her fake breasts nearly getting stuck as I pulled her out.

"I've been calling you for days," she said, her face badly bruised. She looked like she had been beaten to death. I read her toe tag. He name was Darcy Malone.

"I need to feel your freezing skin against mine," I said, feeling like her voice was coming from my mouth. I climbed on top of the body seeing her smiling face. She licked her lips, and I kissed her, lifting up my hospital gown and letting my erect cock slide into her. Frigid cunt, fuck it felt so tight, the smell of stale piss and perished organs invigorated my nostrils. The rot coated my cock in its liquid embrace. I came like a fountain, filling her with my milk. Spent, I wiped my seed from her, her silence absolute and pushed her back into her chamber.

The meds actually made me able to string a sentence together, albeit a bit disjointed. I had been in the hospital for a few days and the doctor told me I could go home as long as I checked in daily with him. I had to keep a journal of my feelings and was

to have counselling sessions twice weekly until they were satisfied that I was not a danger to myself.

My mom asked Father Gregory if I could help take care of the graveyard, believing it would do me good to be out in the fresh air and not cooped up inside surrounded by corpses.

On a mild day I began weeding the flowerbeds at the side of the church.

"I'm sorry to hear what happened to you son, but you know that God will always be there for you should you need him." I nodded sharply and began digging little holes to put the bedding plants in. I did like being outside and the graveyard felt familiar and relaxing. I felt like Amelia was with me.

"You have been a Godsend." Father Gregory said taking out a plant from its plastic and handing me it. "This cemetery is a lot for Max to take care of on his own." Max did fuck all especially now I was helping. He just liked to dig the graves and fuck off home.

The pills were supposed to make me calmer, and they did, but it seems that they amplified the mumblings of the dead.

I took the wheelbarrow to the place near the old mausoleums to prune some bushes. There were five grand old tombs there, one of which was from a Victorian family called the Argents who were all buried there together. I heard giggling and singing

from behind the tomb door. The opening was ornate with an angel in flight as a figurehead over the top. I tried the door, and it wouldn't budge.

"Come and play, come and dance," said the lilting voice. I used the point of the shears against the door mechanism, and it creaked a little. I pushed and after a couple of minutes the corroded metal split and I heard a joyful cheer from within. I pulled open the door hearing it scrape on the floor. It was quite dark inside the tomb, the only light coming from the half-moon-stained glass windows near the ceiling, casting orange and green shadows onto the floor. There were four coffins on stone shelves. In the middle of the tomb was a statue of a weeping angel. The giggling intensified and I went to one of the coffins breaking the perished wood with the shears. A skeleton arm draped out.

"Help me Bryce," the skeleton said so I pulled the rest of the wood away and took the remains out of their resting place. She stood up, dressed in the remnants of a gown and wrapped her arms around my neck.

"Dance with me." The skeleton began to sing a jaunty rhyme. "*Come, come and make eyes at me down at the Old Bull and Bush.*" We began to waltz, the vivid colours of the stained glass lighting our performance. She put her bony hand on my cock. I unzipped and freed my meat, letting her skeletal hand wank me off. She was still singing merrily, her mouth dropping on to the tip of my dick

every so often, teasing me.

"Jesus fucking Christ!" I turned my head and saw Max in the doorway. "I heard singing. What the fuck are you doing with that skeleton?!" Talk about a buzz kill. I stood up.

"Did you really hear singing?" I said, my dick wagging with a blood engorged erection.

"Yes! That's why I came to look. You sick fuck! You shouldn't mess with the dead. That's desecration of the departed. I'm going to tell Father Gregory and your parents."

"Hey Max," I said picking up the shears, "you forgot something." Max turned and I impaled his gut. He looked stunned then he fell to the stone floor gurgling. I pulled the shears out, the blood splattering onto my cock. I rammed the shears a couple more times into his back for good measure. I had to make sure he was dead. Then I dragged the body into the corner and left it there. I heard the rattling of bones from the other coffins as if in applause of my actions. My dancing partner was lay on the floor moaning for me to finish in her mouth. I sat over the skull and shoved my dick into the open orifice pumping and smashing the skull into smithereens until the splinters were mixed with my ejaculation. The now skull-less skeleton lay abandoned. I left the tomb and closed the door, getting back to my pruning.

8 MOMMY'S BOY

Father Gregory and I stood and watched as the camera guy wired up cameras on various lamp posts around the cemetery. That would be difficult if women in the graveyard began calling to be fucked. I'd have to make sure I was out of the line of sight.

"That lazy son of a bitch hasn't turned up in three days!" Father Gregory complained, "I'm going to have to find someone else to dig the graves."

"I can do it if you show me how to use the digger," I said, beginning to sweep the church steps.

"Bryce that would really help me out. We have two funerals this week and I don't think I'll find someone at such short notice." So, Father Gregory gave me a crash course on operating the excavator. I had to go to a newer part of the cemetery to dig a hole for tomorrow. The female occupant of this hole was in our mortuary. The deeper I dug, the more I could hear her telling me how gaping her cunt was for my dick. I was hard by the time I finished and parked up the digger next to the shed. I rubbed my erection, knowing I was going to have to wait until father had gone home. It was only 3pm and I still had some planting to do near the cemetery gates. I weeded the bed and raked the soil ready for the bulbs. It was difficult with a stonking erection, and I knew I needed to empty my balls and soon. I cleared up and went to tell Father Gregory I was

done for the day. Much as I loved my outdoor labour, I longed for the smell of corpses. I entered the church; the aroma of candle wax and bibles filled the air. Father Gregory was sat at the front pew with Theresa Goodman, the butcher's daughter. She was giggling as he handed her a chocolate bar. My blood went cold. Why was she here alone in the church? Where were her parents?

Father Gregory heard my footsteps and turned sharply, like I had caught him about to commit a heinous act.

"Ah Bryce… You know Theresa? She is going to read a passage in church this Sunday."

Theresa beamed at me; her face covered in melted chocolate.

"Hey Bryce," she said, happily, "do you want a piece?"

"No thanks. Can't be spoiling my appetite. Mom will go crazy if I don't eat dinner." I turned to Father Gregory. "I'm finished for the day. See you tomorrow." He smiled, looking like a python ready to eat a mouse. I didn't want to leave Theresa there with him, but what else could I do? The Father had given me an opportunity to heal my mind by working in the graveyard, so I couldn't go ahead and accuse him. But I didn't like it. I made a mental note to check on Theresa later.

I went to the funeral parlour and father was just

finishing up.

“Is this the person that’s being buried tomorrow?” I asked, staring at the middle-aged woman who was grinning at me and touching her nipples.

“Yes. How are you son?” My dad was actually being warm towards me.

“I’m doing OK, but I miss working with you dad.” I said, feeling my dick getting hard again.

“Maybe you can come back a couple of days a week until all of this calms down,” he said, washing the blood off his hands. I stared at the corpse.

“Lick my cunt,” it said, wiggling its tongue.

“What did you say Bryce?!” said my dad, alarmed.

“You, You heard her?” I said, incredulous.

“Heard who?” My father said, worry creeping across his face.

“Nothing-never mind. I miss Amelia,” I said, swiftly changing the subject.

“We all do son,” He said, sadly, clasping my shoulder.

“Do you want me to vacuum the chapel and see to the flowers?” I asked, needing to fuck this woman so she’d stop tormenting me.

"Are you sure? I don't want your mom to get on my back for making you work too much instead of relaxing and getting better." Dad said, taking off his apron.

"I want to. I just want to get back to some normality." I smiled wanly.

"Well, if you're sure. I need to go and see Father Gregory anyway before dinner." My dad left quick sharp. Whatever it was must be urgent. If only he knew the real reason I was here.

The woman opened her legs. She wasn't a looker, but her cunt would do to satisfy my burning cock.

"I thought he'd never leave," she said, blood dribbling out of her mouth. I pulled the sheet from her body and saw that she was covered in burns. The skin was barely held together, even with my father's expert sewing.

"I hope you like the pussy well done!" she chortled, and I undressed and flung my length into her, fucking the wadding as well which was sopping wet and full of pus and congealed blood. She began to scream, and I grabbed her hips and delved in up to the balls, my ravenous penis gorging on her decomposing innards.

I heard another piercing scream; one I was familiar with. My mother's cry.

"Bryce, what are you doing?!" She dropped the

funeral wreath she had been carrying. “I heard the moaning and thought your father had injured himself,” she said, in shock.

“OOPS! Momma’s here, no more fucking for you, you naughty boy. Now she knows your filthy secret,” cackled the corpse.

“Oh my boy, it’s worse than they said,” mom said, devastated. She began to cry.

“You can hear her too?” I said, amazed. “Are you special too?”

“It’s you Bryce. It was your voice. It sounds like you are putting on a woman’s voice, but no, it’s you speaking,” mom whimpered, choking on her tears. She looked like she was going to be sick. I got off the body, the intestines spilling out from the suture that had ripped open with my hard fucking. Silently I wiped my cock and got dressed. My mom backed away from me, her body shaking with sobs.

“Where’s your father? I think we need to have a family talk,” she said, edging towards the door.

“It wasn’t me speaking mom, it was them. Can’t you hear them all? The voices from the graveyard, the mortuary room, the crypts. They never let me rest. It’s real, it’s not in my head!!” I began to punch myself in the temple, trying to stop the noise, hoping mom could hear them too.

“Kill her!” screamed the corpse, “or you will be

locked away and never be able to have fun anymore!"

"Oh God Bryce, please! It's OK," appeased my mom," we can call the doctor, we will get you better!" I clawed at my face and slapped it, my nails slicing the skin causing the lacerations to bleed.

"There's nothing wrong with me mom! I was chosen to be able to hear them. They need me!" I picked up a trocar off the metal trolley and, taken over by my feral rage and need to protect my double life at all costs, I lunged at my mother and shoved the needle like tool into her eye. She howled in pain and the blood gushed down her face.

"Please stop!" She staggered and I hit her over the head with the fire extinguisher off the wall, pounding her skull until there was nothing left but shards of bone and lumpy brain matter.

"Well done my boy," said the corpse approvingly. I didn't care that I had just killed my mom. There was no way I could hear these voices without acting on them and living out my carnal desires. If I didn't I would scratch my eyes out.

Then I heard her- Amelia.

"Bryce, Bryce where are you?" I ran out of the mortuary covered in mom's brains and went to Amelia's grave. She was shouting now.

"Let me out! It's dark in here. I'm scared."

"Don't worry Amelia, I'm coming!" I pulled the excavator keys out of my pocket, jumped in and pumped the gas as fast as it would allow and drove to dig up my sister, not giving a fuck if I was caught on Father Gregory's snazzy new cameras.

"Hurry Bryce! I can't breathe!"

"It's OK I've got you, big brother's here."

9 THE CHAMBER

Mason had been talking to Father Gregory about my escapades at his brothel and after some convincing, the priest had decided to let me see his chamber beneath the church. All day I had been nursing a semi hard cock, chomping at the bit for the delights that I was going to see.

The church door was on the latch, and I made my way down the stone steps behind a wooded door at the back of the altar concealed by an ornate tapestry. All was as he said it would be. It smelt like wet earth the deeper I went down, feeling like I was travelling to another world, a world of sin and malice. I heard the screaming, high pitched and terrified. I took the first door a little down the tunnel. My eyes were assaulted by an onslaught of depravity. Machines of all manner of pain were set up around the room and there was a big rickety old table covered in dried blood displaying many

machines?" I said, grimacing at the vinegar like quality of the wine.

"I do. I look at old Medieval torture devices and then add my own spin on it. You know, we could use you to help get the kids to Mason's. Saves me having to drive them. Then I can concentrate on my affairs here and you are less conspicuous."

"Sure," I said, excited to be involved in this perverted business, "I'm there a lot anyway. I'm sure we can sort something out."

"We will reward you greatly for your troubles of course. Anything you like- money or flesh," Father Gregory said, draining his chalice and refilling it.

"Well can we get on with it and fuck Theresa once more? I'm going to have to get home soon," I said, checking my watch, "or Valerie will wonder where I am."

"Of course. By the way your son has been such a big help since Max has gone AWOL. Great boy you have there Eddie," Father Gregory smiled.

"He's getting there," I said, genuinely proud of my son, "I just hope he can finally turn a corner and we can try and mend our broken family."

"You know, you would have succumbed eventually. If Amelia hadn't died you would have fucked her and broken your family yourself. Once the devil's seed is planted it can only flourish," Father Gregory

mused.

We untied Theresa who flopped limply over Father Gregory's shoulder and took her to the leather sling. After she was in place we stood one by her ass and one by her face and rammed our hard cocks in her openings.

"Yes Amelia," I said, gazing through bleary eyes as I felt my orgasm rise, "choke on daddy's spunk."

The devil had his claws deep within me now.

10 ANNIHILATION

"Nearly there Bryce! Open the coffin!" yelled Amelia. I jumped into the grave and used my spade to prise open the lid. I was jubilant to find Amelia laying there smiling at me. She looked a bit grey, but it was still her dressed in her pretty dress with the bows on it- one of her favourites. I picked her up and cradled her close, my tears running freely.

"I can't do this without you. The voices, they came back stronger. I need you." I said into her hair.

"I'm here now let's go home," she said, hugging me tightly. I lifted her above my head and out of the hole and then I pulled myself out, nearly slipping on the disturbed earth. I picked her up and headed towards the church.

"Why are we going to the church? I want to see mommy," she said, pouting.

“Mommy’s gone baby. I want Father Gregory to see that you are alive. That death is just an illusion,” I said, determination in my voice.

“But Bryce, only you can see and hear me,” Amelia said, gravely.

“Mommy saw the woman in the mortuary, I know she did,” I said, defiantly. I made my way into the church and sat Amelia in one of the pews. I saw the tapestry on the wall behind the altar flapping in the breeze. Curious, I went to take a look and saw a half open door, behind which was a stone staircase. I went downstairs. I heard a girl’s cry and the primal grunting of men. I threw open the door and saw Theresa being violated by Father Gregory and my dad. I vomited, then got angry when I heard my dad call her Amelia as he ejaculated into her mouth. She coughed and spluttered.

“Amelia is upstairs,” I said, startling both of them. Father Gregory the dirty old bastard and my own dad- a pair of paedophiles. I was burning with rage. I frantically looked around the chamber of horrors and snatched a metal hook with someone’s dried blood on it off the table. With it I hooked Father Gregory up the ass. He squealed like a skewered pig, and I pulled him off the floor, the grafting I had been doing in the churchyard had definitely improved my muscular strength. I flung the priest into the corner seeing the blood gurgling from his asshole and mouth. He coughed up lumps and

floundered, trying to remove the hook. Dad darted at me, but I dodged him.

“You of all people preaching about the goodness of life and how I should be living and learning when you are here hurting kids. You fucking hypocrite. I am no longer your son,” I sneered and jumped on him, beating his face with my bare fists. “You were going to hurt Amelia weren’t you? Well now I’m going to stop you from hurting anyone ever again!” I shrieked. My dad was no match for my furious rampage, and I smashed his head into the stone floor repeatedly until I heard a crack. Blood pumped out of his splintered skull, and he was blubbering.

“I’m sorry, I’m sorry….”

“Save it for God!” I yelled and spat on him. My attention turned back to Father Gregory who had dragged himself along the floor leaving a bloody trail behind him and had grabbed a wooden mallet from the table.

“Haha!! What are you going to do with that?!” I kicked him in the head, and he dropped the mallet with a resounding thud. I dragged him to the two metal shackles on the wall and secured him, his shrivelled cock wagging. He was sweating and babbling to himself, the hook still embedded in his rectum. I grabbed a pair of mole grips from the gruesome array of goodies and clamped them around his cock. Then I pulled. He projectile vomited all over me. I laughed stupidly, carrying on

pulling and twisting. Then the cock began to split locked tight in the jaws of the mole grips. Father Gregory bellowed in pain as his dick separated from his body. Blood sprayed out like a burst water main.

“I’m coming Charlie,” he whispered, his eyes flickering.

“Good luck explaining all of this to God,” I said, lifting Theresa out of the sling and wrapping her in Father Gregory’s robes.

“Come on, let’s go and get Amelia,” I whispered, walking back upstairs.

“But isn’t Amelia dead?” murmured Theresa, her voice hoarse.

“Not to me. I can’t hear them now.”

I sat in the pew cuddling Amelia whilst Theresa curled up into a ball and sobbed.

11 REUNITED

The sirens peeled through the churchyard, and I was vaguely aware of Theresa's parents comforting her. They had become worried when Father Gregory hadn't walked her home and when they discovered us, her father called the cops. They were storming the church now and I felt very far away somewhere safe with Amelia.

"Bryce, Bryce!" Theresa's mother snapped me out of my trance, "thank you for saving our daughter." Her face was grief stricken and alarmed seeing me sat there covered in vomit, blood and soil cradling my dead sister. They left and took Theresa to the waiting ambulance.

"Jesus Christ!" I heard one of the policemen say. "You've got to see what's down here." They all went down to the torture room. Hopefully Father Gregory

and my father were dead by now.

“Son, son come on you need to let go of her.” A gentle faced paramedic tried to take Amelia from me. I gripped her harder.

“It’s OK,” she said, “I will wait for you.” The paramedic looked at me in both sadness and perverse curiosity as I gave him Amelia’s body.

A policewoman sat next to me then and began asking questions. I held up my hand wearily.

“I did it. I killed my dad and Father Gregory when I saw them hurting Theresa. And, if you look in the mortuary you will find my mom’s body and in the old Argent crypt Max’s body. I killed them all.”

Silently, I let her cuff me and lead me away. Because I was no longer with Amelia, the voices returned, lamenting my departure.

I really couldn’t be bothered having endless interviews and interrogations, so I signed a confession for all four murders. They could understand why I killed Father Gregory and my dad and secretly I think they were glad that I’d disposed of two child predators. When they searched our house they found three hard drives behind a false wall in the attic full of child pornography. There was also a duffel bag containing soiled children’s underwear. Father Gregory’s catacombs had the remains of around twenty kids in various stages of decomposition in the pit. The police were baffled as

to why he had started to torture kids and the blood stains proved there had been way more than twenty persecuted here, so what had happened to the rest of them? Unfortunately no one was left alive to answer that question.

Max and my mom were innocent parties in all of this, and the officers thought it was downright cruel of me to take my mom's life after she had just lost her daughter. I told them the voices made me or everyone would find out what I did. I never revealed to them my penchant for fucking corpses, they just thought I was referring to killing people.

My broken mind led me to be institutionalised at Trinity Heights Psychiatric Hospital. To be honest, it wasn't that bad. It was a relatively modern place on a bluff along the coast. After six months in the high security wing without incident, I was released into gen pop and given my own bedroom. The gardens gave a stunning view of the sea and I spent most of my time there tending to the flower beds. I no longer heard voices and the meds they gave me made me feel pretty chipper. I was however frightfully lonely. I missed my parents, even dear old dad. I had just wanted a normal life. Why had my dad been such a vile cretin? I did feel guilty every day for killing my mom. The rest of my extended family just wished I was the one who was dead since I was a psychopathic murderer. I did have cravings. I missed the feel of dead skin, so I began to paint; violent, haunting images of dead

women in various raunchy poses with open rotted pussies and decomposed faces. My doctor said I'd never be let out if I kept painting horrific art, but another patient's relative who had an Avant Garde gallery in the next town saw my paintings and wanted to buy them.

"You are an amazing artist. I can feel the pain and eroticism in these paintings. Bravo!" He said, excitedly, so he bought the whole collection, much to the dismay of my doctor. I suppose people who harbour locked away feelings express themselves strongly through imagery. It became my therapy and further ensured that the voices wouldn't return. I thought that I was going to be able to live my life in some semblance of peace, but I was sadly mistaken.

A new female patient arrived who was taken to the high security wing. I heard her screaming and swearing as she was brought in. She was covered in cuts and bruises and apparently she had beaten her two children to death after her husband ran off with her sister, then had tried to commit suicide by throwing herself down three flights of stairs. Miraculously, she didn't break any bones. She lasted two days before she overpowered one of the orderlies and smashed him over the head with a chair. Then she used his belt to hang herself. I heard her calling to me the following evening from the basement of the hospital. I was so annoyed that the voices had come back. I thought I was cured.

"Please Bryce, please come and console me. I need a gentle touch. I'm hurting, I need to feel pleasure. I can no longer bear the pain," she cried desperately.

I left my room, taking care not to bump into the night nurses during their rounds. I slipped into the elevator and cruised down to the morgue. I could hear her screaming.

"Help me! Save me! Fuck me!" I knew deep down it was me saying those words. On refection during my time in here, I had realised that I was borderline insane. I flicked on the lights. The morgue was very up to date and painfully clinical. She was on a slab uncovered. Her head turned and looked at me, her neck a vibrant purple and green colour.

"My cunt wants you baby. Eat me!" she demanded, opening her legs. I gazed longingly at her black wiry muff. I didn't want to do this anymore. I was here with these voices in my head, being commanded by the dead, tortured by them. I smacked myself in the head wanting this anguish to end. The woman was pleading with me now, but I was no longer the devil's puppet. I picked up a scalpel off the medical trolley and for the first time I felt in control of my actions. I slowly and deeply scored it along my throat. I slid to the floor, blood spurting out over my pyjamas. The voice of the corpse was still coming out of my mouth telling me to stop. But then I heard another voice.

"It's OK Bryce. There's no more pain now." My eyes flickered. I was sure it was a hallucination because my life was slipping away, but there she was, heaven's light surrounding her, as vibrant and angelic as I remember her. My Amelia.

"Come on, let's go away from here," she said, bathing me in her warm light.

"But Amelia, I won't be able to go to heaven after what I've done," I said, suddenly frightened.

"We're not going to heaven silly. We are going somewhere else where we can have picnics and do fun things all day. Just you and me big brother."

I glanced back at my dead body and shuddered. Amelia took my hand, and we walked through the blinding light to the other place where I would never be tormented again.

EPILOGUE

Two years later…

“Come on Martin! I dare you to go into the basement! That’s where Father Gregory killed all the kids. They say he stalks the catacombs looking for his next victim.”

Martin shook with fear and rubbed his knees where he had grazed them as they climbed over the locked cemetery gates. The graveyard was badly overgrown, and the old house was boarded up after what had happened there. All of the murders and the scandal surrounding the dirty old child killing vicar, meant that no one wanted to go near this place. It was left to rot and decay. A symbol of fear and material for ghost stories to scare the local children. There was talk of moving the bodies up to a new church that was being built, but none of that had come to fruition.

"Go on you chicken!" Martin opened the church door, surprised it wasn't bolted. Inside it was pretty dark and dust clouds hung in the air. He tiptoed to the altar where it was rumoured was the door to the catacombs. Sure enough, there it was. He peered around the door frame.

"Boo!" yelled Liam, his friend, making him jump out of his skin. The other three boys howled with laughter, jabbing him in the ribs to go down. He turned on his torch and descended the stone steps. He could hear crying halfway down and backed up a couple of steps.

"Someone is down there!" he said, quivering with fear. He turned to run back up, but instead of bumping into his friends he was faced with a decomposed vicar with half his face missing.

Martin screamed as Father Gregory enveloped him in darkness.

DUG UP

Printed in Dunstable, United Kingdom

66036696R00057